I0608247

Saturday Popular Concerts.

DIRECTOR—Mr. S. ARTHUR CHAPPELL

Four Hundred and Ninety-ninth Concert.*

PROGRAMME FROM THE WORKS OF

Various Masters.

SATURDAY AFTERNOON, JANUARY 18th, 1873

QUINTET, in C minor, for two Violins, two Violas,
and Violoncello.   *Mozart*

(Second performance at the Popular Concerts.)

Allegro—C minor.
Andante—E flat major.
Minuet—C minor; with Trio—C major.
Allegro (finale)—C minor and major.

Herr STRAUS, Herr L. RIES, Mr. ZERBINI,
Mr. BURNETT, and Signor PIATTI.

This, the third of Mozart's string quintets, was composed
at Vienna, in 1782, as a serenade for eight wind instruments
(two oboes, two clarinets, two horns, and two bassoons,) and
in 1783-4 arranged by Mozart himself in the form presented
to-day. It is one of the prolific master's most beautiful
compositions, but throughout so clear and simple in plan, that
to do anything more than cite the principal themes in each
movement would be superfluous.

* Fourteenth Concert of the Seventeenth Season.

479

Allegro (first theme).

(Second theme.)

1st Violin and 1st Viola.

2nd Violin.

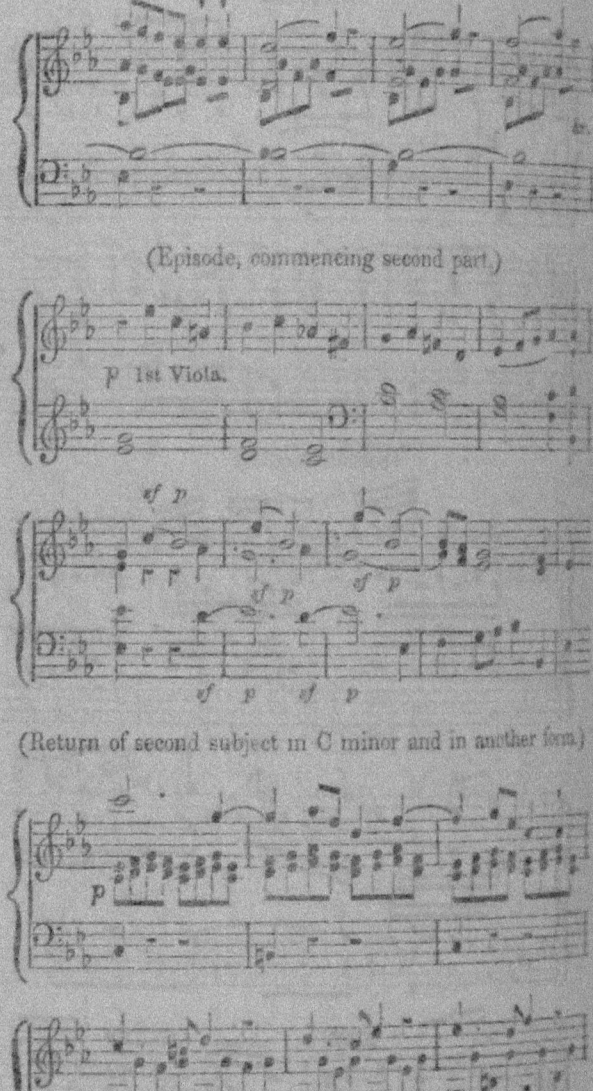

(Episode, commencing second part.)

P 1st Viola.

sf p

sf p

sf p

sf p sf p

(Return of second subject in C minor and in another form.)

P

481

Andante.

(Second theme.)

&c

Minuetto.

This *minuetto* is in the form of a canon on the octave between treble and bass, with harmony in the other parts.

Trio.

1st Violin.

Cello.

This is what the Italians term "*canone al rovescio*," in which the subject is answered by inversion.

Finale (Theme).

This *finale* is in the form of an air with variations; but it contains an episode, which may be indicated by a very few bars :—

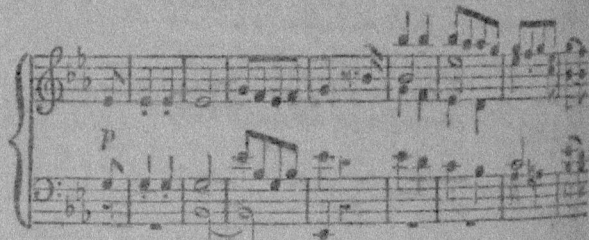

The last variation, in the major key, forms also the coda.

The Quintet in C minor was first introduced by Herr Joachim, Herr L. Ries, Mr. H. Blagrove, Mr. Zerbini, and Signor Piatti, at the fourteenth concert of the eleventh season —February 8, 1869.

SONG, Miss ANNIE SINCLAIR.   *Handel.*

(*L'Allegro.*)

If I give thee honour due,
Mirth, admit me of thy crew,

SONG.

Let me wander, not unseen,
By hedge-row elms on hillocks green;
Where the ploughman, near at hand,
Whistles o'er the furrow'd land;
And the milk-maid singeth blithe,
And the mower whets his scythe;
And ev'ry shepherd tells his tale
Under the hawthorn in the dale.
Or let the merry bells ring round,
And the jocund rebecks sound
To many a youth and many a maid
Dancing in the checquer'd shade.

GRAND SONATA, in F minor, Op. 57, for Pianoforte alone.* *Beethoven.*

(Sixteenth performance at the Popular Concerts.)

Allegro assai—F minor.
Andante con moto—D flat major.
Allegro ma non troppo } —F minor.
Presto.

Madlle. MARIE KREBS.

The second of the three "*colossi*"—alluded to in the remarks upon the Sonata, Op. 53, dedicated to Count Waldstein—this remarkable composition was inscribed to Francis Count of Brunswick. Ferdinand Ries (the well-known pianist and composer, for some years Beethoven's pupil) relates an anecdote in connection with the last movement, which, as thoroughly characteristic of the great "tone-poet," is worth reproducing. During a walk in the country, they (Ries and Beethoven) had wandered from the ordinary road. All the way, Beethoven had been doing nothing but sing, or rather, howl, the scale from top to bottom, without once articulating a note distinctly. "I have found a subject," he said, "at last." No sooner home, than, rushing to the pianoforte, even without taking off his hat, Beethoven revelled for an hour uninterruptedly in what afterwards took the shape of the magnificent *finale* of the Sonata, Op. 57. Cranz, a music publisher at Hamburgh—the same who christened the Sonata in D, Op. 28, *Sonata Pastorale*—was the first to entitle the sonata, Op. 57, *Sonata Appassionata*, a nomenclature of which Beethoven himself was incognizant. The name has since, however, been generally associated with the work.

The first movement has a leading theme so striking and impassioned, that none could doubt the use that would be made of it by such a poetical musician as Beethoven :—

---

* No. 23 of Beethoven's Sonatas, edited by Mr. Charles Hallé —published by Messrs. Chappell and Co. 50, New Bond Street.

A repetition of this—half a tone higher :—

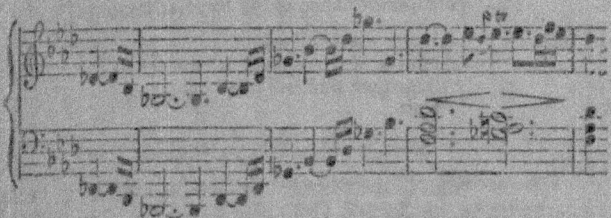

—is a master-stroke, the major key even enhancing the expressive character of the melody. The mysterious relation (of which Beethoven so well knew the secret) between the harmony of the tonic and that of the minor second of the scale, never received a more powerful illustration. The pause on the first inversion of the dominant harmony of F minor, ( ) by which this is immediately followed :—

brings us back again to the exact point at which we were before—so as, it would seem, to render the intervening bars superfluous. Beethoven, however, makes use of it as pretext for a *point d'orgue* and *cadenza di bravura*, which, pausing at length on the same inversion of the dominant harmony:—

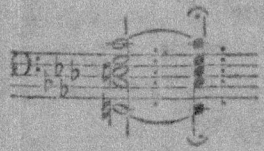

gives way to a further development of the leading theme after a new fashion :—

At last, as if tired of the continuous reappearance of this same chord, (*) Beethoven, with an unceremoniousness peculiar to him, suddenly quits it for the dominant seventh (*) of the key in which the second subject is to appear :—

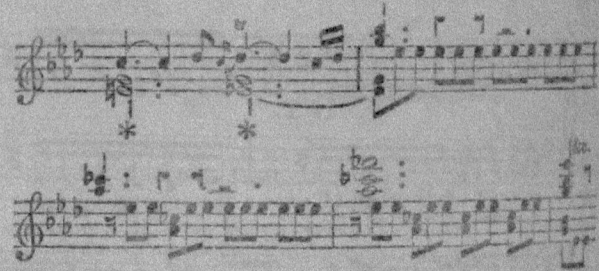

The foregoing is merely a prelude to the tranquil and expressive melody of the second subject proper (in A flat major), a melody invested with a serene dignity through which its beauty shines resplendent :—

A beautiful transition :—

—which a *cadenza*, on the dominant, rounds off into completeness—leads us back once more to A flat (now minor), with a new and characteristic idea :—

The working out of the foregoing brings the first part to a conclusion, in A flat minor. There is no "repeat;" but, with a bold, enharmonic transition, the elaborations of the second part are thus summarily ushered in :—

The beauties of this second part, in which the chief materials already cited are varied, developed, and combined with new matter in a "free *fantasia*," sparkling and glowing with traits of imagination, must be heard to be appreciated. An indication or two may suffice as guiding points. Here is a prelude :—

Second time an octave higher.

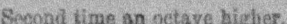

—which prepares the way for an episode, constructed upon the leading feature of the principal theme :—

Here another, scarcely less expressive, introducing the
second subject in a fresh key (D flat):—

After a series of interesting progressions, of which xam-
ples are subjoined:—

—the theme is again abandoned for a brilliant and extended *cadenza*, in " arpeggios," built upon the dominant harmony, which ultimately brings about the resumption of the principal subject. This, however, comes in unexpectedly before the pedal upon which the *cadenza* is built is relinquished:—

—and it is not until the continuation of the leading theme re-appears—now in the major instead of the minor—that the dominant pedal is relinquished and a full close in the key of F attained:—

The remainder, allowing for the necessary change of key, is now a recapitulation, more or less exact, of the first part, until we arrive at the *coda*, through the subjoined mysterious *début* :—

In this *coda* a new and striking "*cadenza alla bravura*" is introduced, the character of which may be suggested by a fragment :—

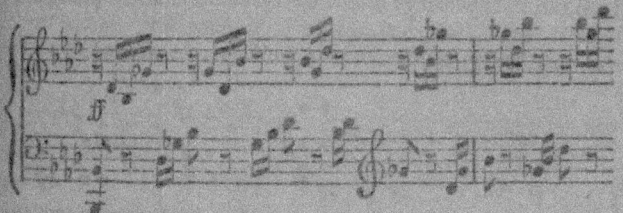

This, after a lengthened development, the climax of which is another *cadenza di bravura*, more brilliant than its precursors, subsides eventually upon the dominant of F minor :—

—and both the original key and the leading theme are resumed, the following modification being one of the most interesting features of its new melodic treatment :—

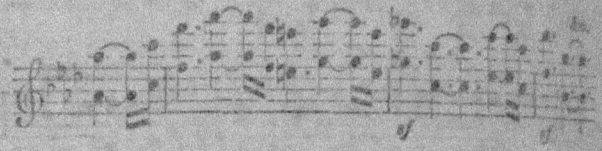

Inspiration never failing, Beethoven is unable (or unwilling) to terminate his *coda* without something that has not been heard before :—

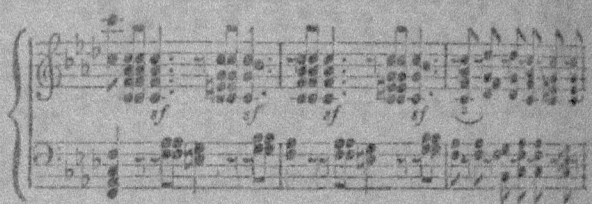

To the foregoing episode succeeds another reference to the leading theme, which, by means of a gradual *diminuendo* from "*fortissimo*" to "*pianissimo*," brings this superb *allegro* to a close.

The *Andante con moto* (D flat)—an air with variations, if not equal in abstract musical beauty to the *allegro*, acts at any rate as a charming relief. Subjoined is the first part of the theme :—

The "consecutive fifths," in similar direction, at bars 6, 7—between the bass and an inner part (* *)—are apparently avoided by the notation (B double-flat, instead of A natural), but sound just the same on a keyed instrument. The second part is of like calibre. Variation, No. 1, begins as follows:—

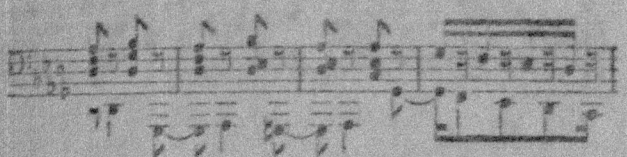

Variation, No. 2, as follows:—

Variation, No. 3, which may be said to form the *coda*, as follows:—

The third variation, being not only developed at greater length, but with greater brilliancy than its predecessor, gives all the more effect to the comparatively unadorned resumption of the theme (*simplex munditiis*):—

The *Andante* does not come to an end, but breaks off—with an interrupted cadence on a discord—as below:—

The *finale*—the wonderful movement to which the anecdote of Ferdinand Ries refers—is announced by a thoroughly dramatic prelude, commencing as subjoined:—

The leading theme affords the key to the whole:—

The continuation, with the melody first in the bass :—

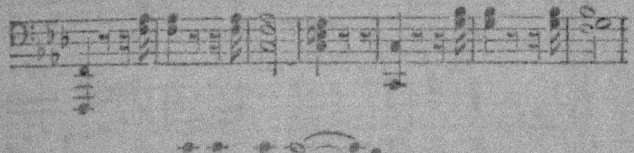

—and then in the treble, each time accompanied in "arpeggios," is thoroughly in keeping. Equally so the very impassioned second subject—

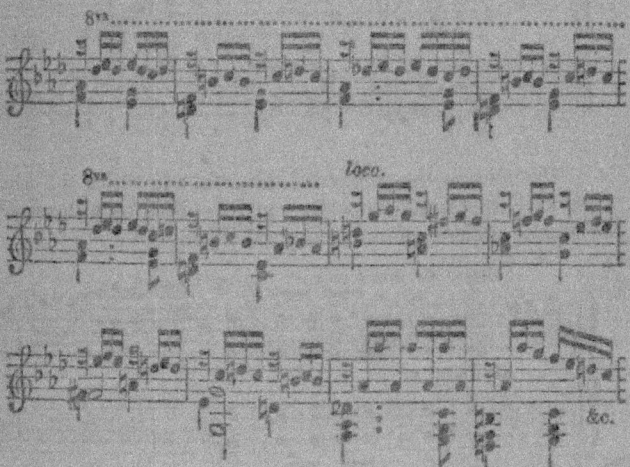

—the further development of which brings us to a full close in C minor, with a fresh allusion to the leading theme in that key :—

Leaving the key of C minor, with a feint of returning to the dominant of F, Beethoven ultimately breaks off upon a discord, and without any "repeat" of the first part, leads at once to the elaborations of the second :—

Among the many striking points in the so-called "free fantasia," may be cited the subjoined :—

—where the right hand echoes the left, and the left again the right, with a singular effect amid so many bustling semi-quavers; and still more characteristic of its author, the following very original and impassioned episode :—

The leading theme with further elaborations (non episodical) is at length resumed in the original key, with the preliminary of a brilliant *cadenza* on the dominant. After one delivery according to the first pattern, it is submitted to a new treatment :—

We have then a recapitulation of the first part (the second subject being now in F minor, instead of C minor); and just at the point where any ordinary composer would have brought his labour to an end, the same discord which arrests the close of the first part and leads to the commencement of the second, now in its turn arrests the close of the second, and brings in a repetition of the whole of it. After the " repeat " (when again the movement might reasonably have ended), we are hurried impetuously into a *coda*, which sets out with this spirited, new, and romantic episode :—

After being given twice as above, the same subject is repeated in the relative major with a striking prolongation of two bars, to bring about the full close in F minor—thus making ten-bar (instead of eight-bar) rhythm (**) :—

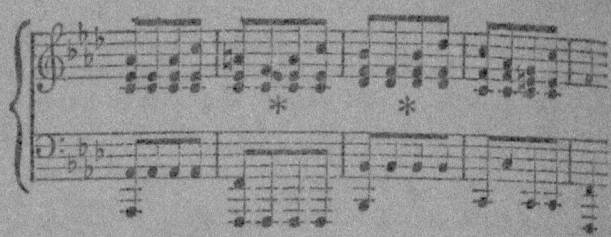

This also is given twice. The principal theme is then taken up and developed in a new fashion, till we come to the peroration :—

—which, ultimately followed up by a series of descending arpeggios, on the harmony of the common chord, leads to a brilliant conclusion one of the finest movements, and one of the finest sonatas to which the great name of Beethoven is attached.

The title of the original edition (advertised in the *Wiener Zeitung*, Feb. 21, 1807) was :—" *LIV*^me *Sonate composée pour Pianoforte et dediée à Monsieur le Comte Francois de Brunswik par Louis van Beethoven. Op. 57. à Vienne au Bureau des Arts et d'Industrie.*" (*Verlags*—*No.* 521. (*Preis 2 fl. 30 kr.*) According to Ries, the sonata was composed in 1804. What is meant by "*LIV*^me *Sonate*" is not easy to guess. Including even the seven early sonatas that in the order of composition precede the three well-known sonatas, Op. 2 (dedicated to Haydn), the *Sonata Apassionata* would still be only the 29th sonata for pianoforte alone.

It was first introduced by Madame Arabella Goddard, at the fourteenth concert of the second season — March 5, 1856.

₊ Madlle. MARIE KREBS will perform on one of Messrs. JOHN BROADWOOD and SONS' Concert Grand Pianofortes.

SATURDAY POPULAR CONCERTS, ST. JAMES'S HALL.—On Saturday afternoon, January 23, the Programme will include Haydn's Quartet in C major, Op. 20, No. 2, for Strings; Hummel's Sonata for Pianoforte and Violoncello, in A major; Beethoven's Sonata in E flat, Op. 12, No. 3, for Pianoforte and Violin; and Beethoven's Sonata in D minor, for Pianoforte alone. Executants, Mdlle. MARIE KREBS, Madame NORMAN-NÉRUDA, MM. STRAUS, L. RIES, and PIATTI. Vocalist, Mr. GREAVES. Conductor, Sir JULIUS BENEDICT. To commence at Three o'Clock.

Subscription Tickets, to the Sofa Stalls, for the 7 Morning Concerts, taking place on Saturdays, January 16, 23, 50, February 6, 13, 20, and 27, at £1 10s.

Sofa Stalls, 5s. Balcony, 3s. Admission, 1s. Tickets and Programmes at CHAPPELL & Co.'s, 50, New Bond Street.

SONATA, in F major, for Violoncello, with Pianoforte
Accompaniment. *Marcello.*

(Second performance at the Popular Concerts.)

Adagio—F major.
Allegro—F major.
Largo—D minor.
Presto—F major.

Signor PIATTI.

(Pianoforte, Sir JULIUS BENEDICT.)

For the pianoforte accompaniment to this sonata we are
indebted to Signor Piatti himself, who has arranged it from
the figured bass of the composer.

Adagio.*

Allegro.*

Largo (D minor).

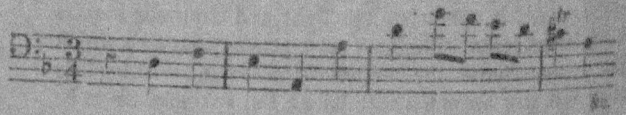

* These movements will be omitted in to-day's performance.

Presto.

&c.

BENEDETTO MARCELLO was born in Venice in 1686, of one of the noblest families of that republic. His musical compositions were very numerous, consisting of psalms, operas, madrigals, and songs. He was also a poet, and wrote several of the dramatic pieces which he set to music. His great work, still well known to musicians, is his *Psalms.* It is a paraphrase of the first fifty Psalms, written by Ascanio Giustiniani, and set to music in one, two, and three vocal parts, by Marcello, published in 1724 and 1725. There is a fine English edition of this work, in eight folio volumes, which was set on foot by Mr. Avison, author of the *Essay on Musical Expression,* and accomplished by Mr. Garth, of Durham, who adapted to the music words from our prose translation of the Psalms. Marcello's Psalms have received more and less than justice from different critics. While Avison's praise is somewhat exaggerated, Burney's censure is too severe. Burney ascribes the "over praise" which Marcello received, partly, at least, to his nobility; but however much this consideration may have operated during his life, it can hardly account for the elevated rank which has been assigned to him as a musician, by the greatest writers on the art. It is enough to mention Padre Martini, of Bologna, who, in his celebrated *Saggio di Contrapunto* (Essay of Counterpoint), mentions Marcello as one of the greatest masters of the Venetian school. The work in question is certainly worthy of the author's reputation. It is full of beautiful and expressive melodies; the contexture of the vocal parts is admirable; and there is great boldness and variety in the modulations and harmonies. The music, however, is somewhat too light and dramatic; it is defective in the severe simplicity and grave solemnity which ought to characterise the ecclesiastical style. Marcello's *Psalms* have now become a rare book; but extracts are to be found in different collections of sacred music; and some movements of them are occasionally heard at concerts.

Among Marcello's literary productions, which are numerous, there is a satire, entitled *Teatro alla moda*, or, "An easy and certain method of composing and performing Italian operas after the modern manner." It is amusing to observe how pointedly the sarcasms against the *modern* fashions of 1720 are applicable to the modes of our own day.

The satire is levelled against poets as well as composers. "The modern poet," says the author, "should completely abstain from reading the ancient writers; for this reason, that the ancient writers never read the moderns. Before entering upon his task, he will take an exact note of the quantity and quality of the scenes which the manager is desirous of introducing into his drama. He will compose his poem verse by verse, without giving himself any trouble as to the action, in order that it may be impossible for the spectator to comprehend the plot, and that curiosity may thus be kept alive to the end of the piece. By the way, he will not forget to close the piece with a brilliant and magnificent scene, terminating in a grand chorus in honour of the sun, the moon, or the manager. He will have recourse as frequently as possible to the dagger, to poison, to earthquakes, spectres, and incantations. All these expedients are admirable; they cost but little, and produce a prodigious effect on the public."

The satirist thus instructs the composer:—"The modern composer has no occasion for a knowledge of the rules of composition; practice, and a few general principles, will be quite sufficient. Nor has he any occasion for an acquaintance with poetry; he need not even be able to distinguish a long syllable from a short one. He will do well *not* to read the poem before setting it to music, for fear of overloading his imagination and oppressing his genius. He will compose the music verse by verse, and will not fail to adjust to the words such airs as he has composed in the course of the year, even though the metre and the expression should be at perfect variance with his ideas. He will produce no airs but such as are accompanied by the whole orchestra; for, in order to compose in the modern taste, it is indispensable above all things to make plenty of noise. As to the singers, they should take care never to practise sol-fa-ing, for fear of falling into the old-fashioned custom of singing in tune and time, both which things are at absolute variance with the taste of the day. And not only will they change the *time* of the airs, but also the airs themselves, though their variations are in direct opposition to the bass and the whole of the instruments."

Any "*laudator temporis acti*" of our own day, wishing to

expose the present vices of the musical stage, in regard to poetry, composition, and performance, would handle the subject exactly as Marcello did above a century ago. He would talk of the degradation of the musical drama by its conversion into a spectacle *full of spectors and incantations;* of the determination of the composers, above all things, *to make plenty of noise;* and of the unmeaning and vicious flourishes with which the airs are loaded by uneducated singers; and he would recall with a sigh, the golden days when the Italian opera flourished in all its beauty and purity. And yet it was in those very golden days that Marcello's satire was written —in the days when Apostolo Zeno was in his zenith, and Metastasio was appearing on the horizon—when the music of the Italian stage was composed by Leo, Vinci, Porpora, Steffani, and Clari, and sung by Faustina, Cuzzoni, Caffarelli, and Farinelli. At a period, too, considerably later, but still at a time when the Italian school retained much of the excellence which it is now universally admitted to have lost, we find, in the correspondence of Metastasio,* the same complaints of the ignorance and bad taste of his contemporaries, and the same regretful looking back to past days, in which Marcello indulged before him, in which we indulge after him, and in which our posterity will indulge after us, so long as human nature shall remain what it is.

Marcello, notwithstanding his devotion to music and poetry, held important offices in the state, and was distinguished for his activity in the discharge of his public duties. He died at Brescia, in 1739.

The Sonata in F major was first introduced by Signor Piatti, at the ninth concert of the seventeenth season—December 7, 1874.

---

* See Burney's *Life of Metastasio.*

SONG, Miss ANNIE SINCLAIR. *Sullivan.*

Orpheus with his lute made trees
And the mountain tops that freeze
  Bow themselves when he did sing:
To his music plants and flow'rs
Ever spring, as sun and show'rs
  There had made a lasting spring.

Ev'ry thing that heard him play,
E'en the billows of the sea,
  Hung their heads when he lay by;
In sweet music in such art,
Killing care and grief of heart,
  Fall asleep, or, hearing, die.

———

TRIO, in C minor, Op. 1, No. 3, for Pianoforte,
Violin, and Violoncello. *Beethoven.*

(Seventh performance at the Popular Concerts.)

Allegro con brio—C minor.
Andante cantabile con variazioni—E flat major.
Menuetto, quasi allegretto—C minor; with Trio—C major.
Finale, prestissimo—C minor.

Madlle. MARIE KREBS, Herr STRAUS, and Signor PIATTI.

The last of the three trios, composed in 1791-2,* which constitute the first published *opus* of Beethoven. These trios were first performed at a *soirée* in the house of the Prince Lichnowski, to which the most noted artists and amateurs of Vienna had been invited. Haydn was present, and every one was anxious to hear his opinion. The great master said much in praise of the new works, but recommended Beethoven not to print the third (the one now introduced). Beethoven, however, considered the Trio in C minor much the best of the set, and from that time is said to have never regarded Haydn with the same cordiality.

The principal themes in each movement of the Trio in C minor are subjoined :—

Allegro con brio (first theme).

---

* Published, and advertised in the *Wiener Zeitung* (Artaria), 19th of March, 1795.

Second theme—relative major.

Andante cantabile (theme).

(First variation—melody only.)

(Second variation.)

(Third variation.)

(Fourth variation—E flat minor.)

(Fifth variation—E flat major.)

un poco più andante.

4 н

(Coda.)

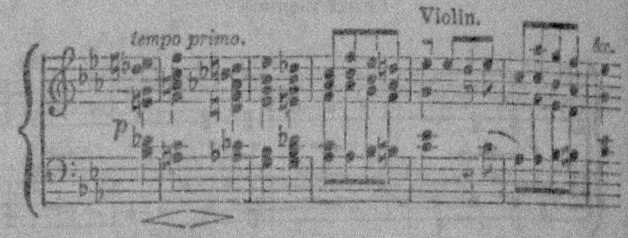

Menuetto quasi allegro.

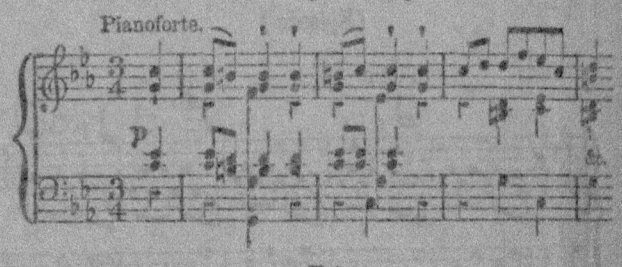

Trio.

Finale (introduction).

511

(First theme.)

(Episode.)

(Second theme.)

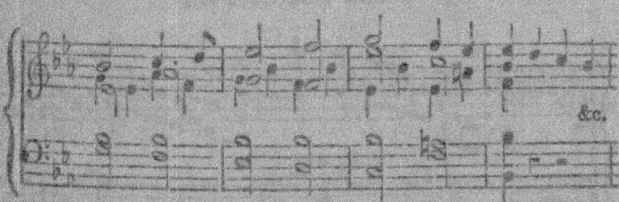

At the house of Prince Lichnowski to whom the three
Trios (Op. 1) were dedicated, and who first instituted the

afterwards celebrated "Rasoumowski Quartet,"* the new compositions of Beethoven used always at one period to be tried. The musician lived under the Prince's roof, and received from him an annual stipend of 600 florins. The princess Lichnowski treated Beethoven like a son, and entertained for him so fond a regard that she often said she would like to keep him under a glass, so that no one might touch him but herself. In what esteem Beethoven was held by certain of the resident aristocracy of Vienna, may be gathered from the fact, that, when, in 1809, Jerome Buonaparte (King of Westphalia) offered him the post of *Kapelmeister*, with a salary of 600 ducats, the Archduke Rodolphe, Prince Kinski, and Prince Lobkowitz (to each of whom the great composer dedicated some of his most important works†) clubbed together and agreed to secure him 4000 florins yearly, provided he would consent to remain in the Austrian dominions—a proposition which Beethoven accepted. Of this annuity, the Archduke paid 1500 florins, Prince Kinski 1800, and Prince Lobkowitz 700. Difficulties subsequently arose, however, which left Beethoven little better off than before.

The Trio in C minor was arranged by the composer as a quartet, and advertised by Artaria as "Op. 104"—Feb. 18, 1819. It was first introduced by Mr. Charles Hallé, Herr Molique, and Herr Lidel, at the tenth concert of the second season—Jan. 30, 1866.

---

* Or "Schupanzig Quartet:" the names of the players being Schupanzig, Sina, Wiess, and Kraft. They are recognized, however, as the "Rasoumowski Quartet," because they were the first to play the three celebrated compositions dedicated to Count Rasoumowski.

† To Prince Kinski, the First Mass (in C), to the Archduke Rodolphe, the famous Trio in B flat and many other works were inscribed; to Prince Lobkowitz, the Six Quartets, Op. 18, &c.

END OF THE FOUR HUNDRED AND NINETY-NINTH CONCERT.

J. MALLETT, PRINTER, 59, WARDOUR STREET, SOHO.

MONDAY POPULAR CONCERTS.

MONDAY EVENING, JANUARY 18th, 1875.

PROGRAMME.

PART I.

QUINTET, in B flat, Op. 87, for two Violins, two Violas,
and Violoncello .... *Mendelssohn.*

Madame NORMAN-NÉRUDA,

MM. L. RIES, STRAUS, ZERBINI, and PIATTI.

TWO-PART SONG, "The Sabbath Morn." .... *Mendelssohn.*

Madlle. NITA GAËTANO and Miss ALICE FAIRMAN.

SONATA, in F minor, Op. 4, for Pianoforte and Violin ... *Mendelssohn.*

Miss AGNES ZIMMERMANN and
Madame NORMAN-NÉRUDA.

PART II.

TEMA con VARIAZIONI, in D, Op. 17, for Pianoforte and
Violoncello .... *Mendelssohn.*

Miss AGNES ZIMMERMANN and Signor PIATTI.

TWO-PART SONG, "I would that my love." .... *Mendelssohn.*

Madlle. NITA GAËTANO and Miss ALICE FAIRMAN.

QUARTET, in D major, Op. 44, No. 1, for two Violins,
Viola, and Violoncello .... *Mendelssohn.*

Madame NORMAN-NÉRUDA,
MM. L. RIES, STRAUS, and PIATTI.

Conductor - Sir JULIUS BENEDICT.

www.ingramcontent.com/pod-product-compliance
Lightning Source LLC
Chambersburg PA
CBHW082051220626
47052CB00006B/1213